LOVE

LOVE

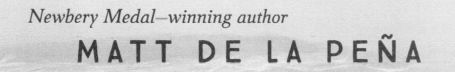

Newbery Medal—winning author
MATT DE LA PEÑA

New York Times *bestselling illustrator*
LOREN LONG

G. P. PUTNAM'S SONS

G. P. Putnam's Sons
an imprint of Penguin Random House LLC
375 Hudson Street
New York, NY 10014

Library of Congress Cataloging-in-Publication Data
Names: de la Peña, Matt, author.
Title: Love / words by Matt de la Peña ; illustrated by Loren Long.
Description: New York, NY : G. P. Putnam's Sons, [2018].
Summary: Illustrations and easy-to-read text celebrate the bonds of love that connect us all.
Identifiers: LCCN 2017016570 | ISBN 9781524740917 (hardback) | ISBN 9781524740931 (ebook)
| ISBN 9781524740924 (ebook) | ISBN 9781524740948 (ebook)
Subjects: | CYAC: Love—Fiction. | Family life—Fiction. | BISAC: JUVENILE FICTION / Social Issues / Emotions & Feelings. | JUVENILE
FICTION / Family / General (see also headings under Social Issues). | JUVENILE FICTION / Social Issues / Values & Virtues.
Classification: LCC PZ7.P3725 Lov 2018 | DDC [E]—dc23
LC record available at https://lccn.loc.gov/2017016570
Manufactured in China by RR Donnelley Asia Printing Solutions Ltd.
ISBN 9781524740917
3 5 7 9 10 8 6 4

Design by Eileen Savage. Text set in Carre Noir Std.
The art was created with collaged monotype prints, acrylic paint and pencil.
Special thanks to Jase Flannery for sharing his vast printmaking knowledge and expertise with me.

For Steven Malk—M. de la P.

For my mother and father,

for a life of love—L.L.

In the beginning there is light
and two wide-eyed figures standing
near the foot of your bed,
and the sound of their voices is love.

A cabdriver plays love softly on his radio

while you bounce in back with the bumps of the city

and everything smells new,
and it smells like life.

Love, too, is the smell of crashing waves, and a train whistling blindly in the distance, and each night the sky above your trailer turns the color of love.

In a crowded concrete park,
you toddle toward summer sprinklers
while older kids skip rope
and run up the slide, and soon
you are running among them,
and the echo of your laughter is love.

On the night the fire alarm blares,
you're pulled from sleep and whisked
into the street, where a quiet old
lady is pointing to the sky.

"Stars shine long after they've flamed
out," she tells you, "and the shine they
shine with is love."

But it's not only stars that flame out, you discover.

It's summers, too.

And friendships.

And people.

One day you find your family
nervously huddled around the TV,
but when you ask what happened,
they answer with silence
and shift between you and the screen.

In your dream that night you are searching
for a love that seems lost.
You open and close drawers,
lift cushions,
empty old toy bins,

but there's nothing.

You wake with a start

in the arms of a loved one

who bends to your ear and whispers,

"It's okay, it's okay, it's love."

And in time you learn to recognize

a love overlooked.

A love that wakes at dawn and

rides to work on the bus.

A slice of burned toast that tastes like love.

And it's love in each deep
crease of your grandfather's face
as he lowers himself onto an
overturned bucket to fish.

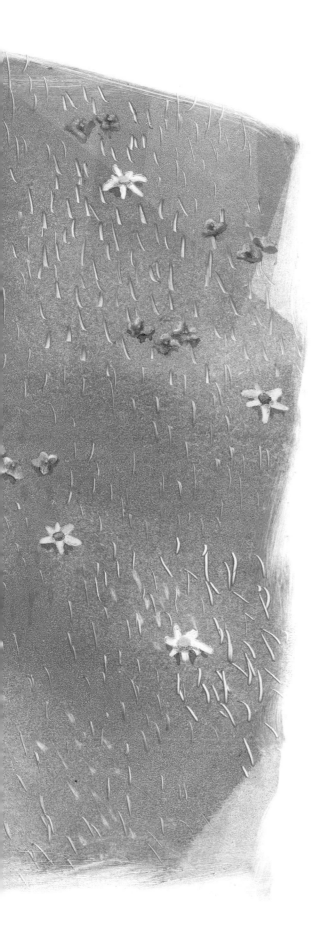

And it's love in the rustling
leaves of gnarled trees
lined behind the flower fields.

And it's love in the made-up stories your uncles tell

in the backyard between wild horseshoe throws.

And the man in rags outside the

subway station plays love notes

that lift into the sky like tiny beacons of light.

And the face staring back
in the bathroom mirror—
this, too, is love.

So when the time comes for you to set off on your own, heavy winds will sweep past your building, and great gray clouds will congregate above.

Your loved ones will stand there like puddles beneath their umbrellas, holding you tight and kissing you and wishing you luck.

But it won't be luck you'll leave with.

Because you'll have love.

You'll have love, love, love.

THIS LOVE
BELONGS TO:

_____